WHAT'S THAT?

Written by Karen Chan
Illustrated by Basia Tran

gloo books

Jaxon had discerning taste. He liked to eat good stuff.
He even ate the things that made some other children huff.

He fancied Camembert and spicy tofu stew.

He also ate green hummus well before he learned to chew.

But what he loved above all else was food his family made,
like tiny dumplings or steamed buns, all twisted in a braid.

Cooking in the kitchen was a special time for Jax,
surrounded by aromas and the sounds of chops and thwacks.

His grandma was an expert chef, so graceful with a knife.
She never needed recipes - she'd been cooking all her life.

She used her hands for every task, to measure, mix and pleat.
And Jax could always count on her to sneak him something sweet.

So when the day arrived for Jax to start at Dapplegray, his grandma cooked her greatest hits, just for his big day.

She packed him tasty lu rou fan, so good it made rice sing,
and added Jax's favorite snack, a chewy cong you bing!

When noon arrived he couldn't wait to eat his homemade treat,
but he noticed other lunches on his way to find a seat.
Everyone had sandwiches, like ham or turkey brie.
No one had a lunch like his as far as he could see.

Mia cheered with Kevin, "Peanut butter is the best!"

Jax began to wish he had the same lunch as the rest.

His food stuck out amid a sea of deli meat and bread.
Then his heart sank deeper when he heard what others said.

Hesitant to eat, he sat there feeling quite alone,

when Meena asked "What's that?" in a kind and eager tone.

Jax described each item, showing Meena this and that.

When it came to things he liked, the boy could really chat.

"We make these pancakes Sundays, just as soon as I'm awake, but not the fluffy kind you stack in layers like a cake.

Nai nai rolls the dough real thin and brushes them with oil.

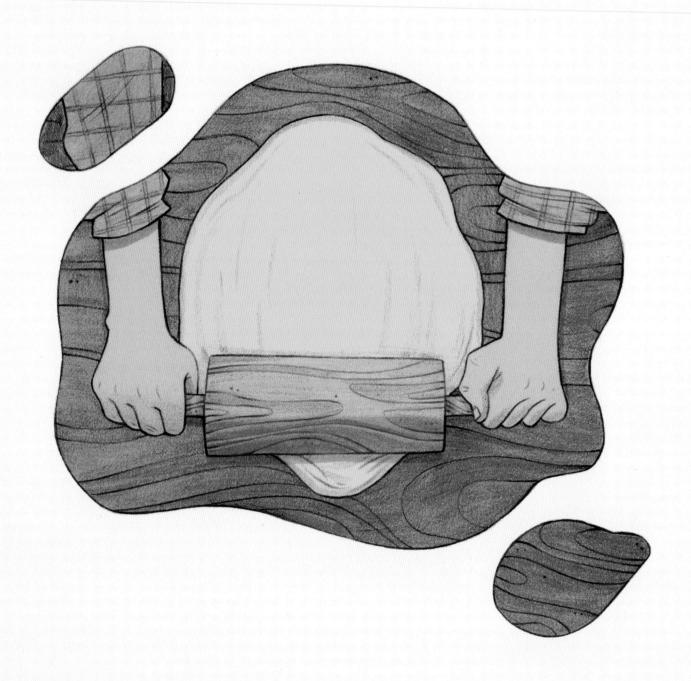

I scatter onions on the top, then shape each in a coil.

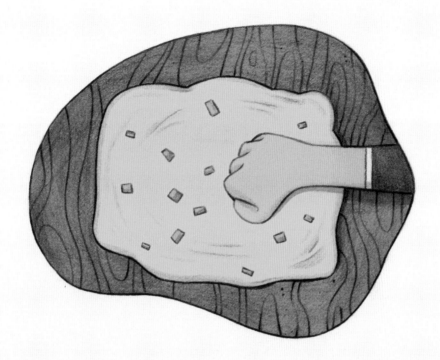

One by one, we cook them in a red-hot frying pan
until each pancake's toasted to a perfect shade of tan."

Meena was surprised. She had a swirly pancake too!
Parathas brushed with ghee had a flaky, buttered chew.

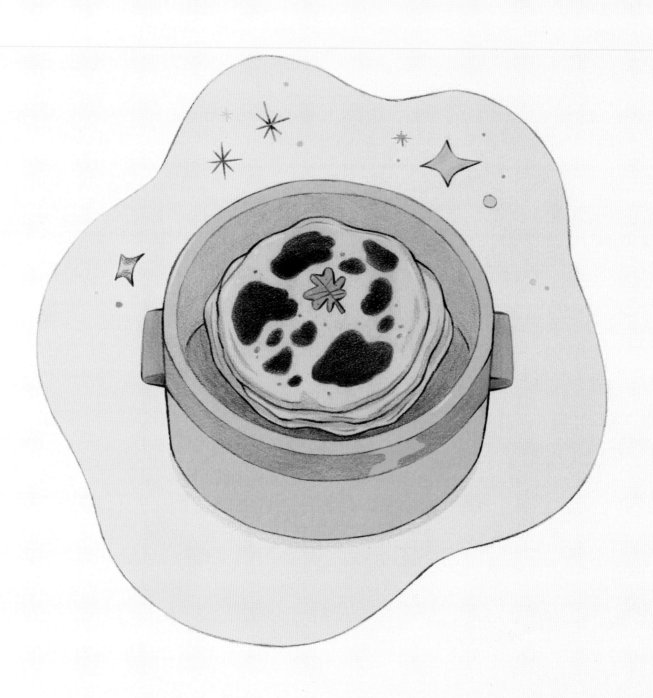

Meena boldly poured some daal atop a mound of rice,
fragrant from some curry leaves and mustard seeds and spice.

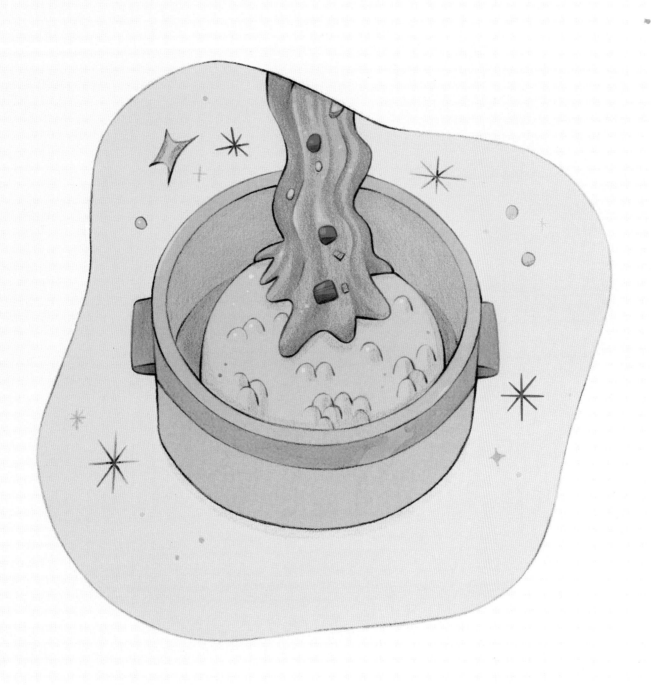

"My favorite times are cooking with my mama in the kitchen. She says sharing food is how we celebrate tradition.

The food we eat is who we are, like clothing, skin or hair."
Then Meena scooped up daal and rice without a single care.

The two continued on with tales of edible delight,
about endless handmade la mian and kulfi pops at night.

And busy chopsticks moving round a steamy, bubbling pot, and the many variations of tangy, crunchy chaat.

And beautiful designs on mooncakes in mid-autumn,
and comfort from a simple bowl of hot and sour rasam.

Although their meals appeared to come from places far apart,
Jax and Meena shared their stories speaking from the heart.

He'd never tried parathas, but indeed Jax understood
how loving hands are all you need to make them taste so good.

Perhaps the food his family ate was not weird after all
but something to eat proudly, just like Meena and her daal.

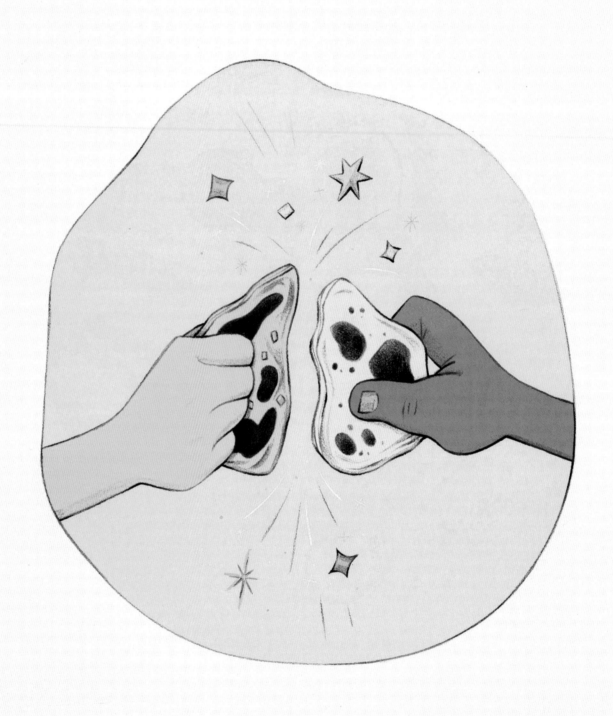

Jax no longer thought about the judgment or the jeers.
And to the foods they cherished, the new friends yelled out

"Cheers!"

Glossary:

चाट CHAAT (CHAHT): This popular snack comes in many different forms. Chaat usually consists of a crispy base served with tangy, savory, sweet and spicy ingredients and topped with a blend of spices called chaat masala.

葱油饼 CONG YOU BING (TZOHNG-YO-BEENG): A pancake with many thin layers filled with green onion. The pancake is pan-fried so that it is crispy and flaky on the outside and chewy on the inside.

दाल DAAL (DAHL): A thick stew or soup made from simmered dried lentils, beans or peas. Daal also refers to the lentil, bean or pea itself.

घी GHEE (GEE): A type of clarified butter used in South Asian cooking.

कुल्फी KULFI (KUHL-FEE): A frozen milk dessert like ice cream that comes in all kinds of flavors.

拉面 LA MIAN (LAH-MYEHN): A flour noodle made by stretching one piece of dough over and over again until the dough becomes long and thin noodles. The noodles are commonly served in a bowl of beef or lamb soup.

卤肉饭 LU ROU FAN (LOO-ROH-FAHN): A stewed pork sauce simmered with soy sauce, ginger and spices like star anise and cinnamon. The sauce is served over rice and usually paired with a soy-marinated egg and vegetables.

奶奶 NAI NAI (NAIH-NAIH): The name for grandmother (father's mother) in Mandarin Chinese.

पराठा PARATHA (PUH-RAH-TAH): A type of flatbread that can be made from different flours and stuffed with different ingredients or eaten plain. The kind that Meena eats is called laccha paratha and is rolled in a unique way so that the bread has thin layers, similar to a cong you bing.

रसम RASAM (RUH-SUM): A spicy and tangy soup often made from tomato, tamarind, chiles and spices like pepper and cumin.

These pronunciations are in Mandarin and Hindi, but there are hundreds of different languages and dialects spoken in the countries where these dishes are eaten!

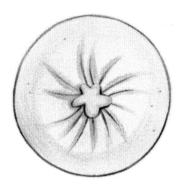

To my family, who taught me that food is love -- K.C.

To my husband Evan, who always shares food with me -- B.T.

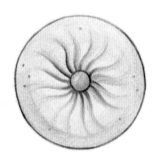

What's That? is published by Gloo Books LLC, 2021

Written by Karen Chan
Illustrated by Basia Tran

The illustrations in this book were rendered in graphite and digitally colored.

For more information or to order books, please visit www.gloobooks.com or contact us at contact@gloobooks.com.

ISBN: 978-1-7372404-0-2

Printed and bound in China.
This book was printed on paper certified according to the standards of the FSC®.

MIX
Paper from
responsible sources
FSC® C017606
FSC
www.fsc.org